EXPOSED
RETRIBUTION

JUDITH GRAVES

ORCA BOOK PUBLISHERS

Library and Archives Canada Cataloguing in Publication

Graves, Judith, author
Exposed / Judith Graves.
(Retribution)

Issued in print and electronic formats.
ISBN 978-1-4598-0722-8 (pbk.).—ISBN 978-1-4598-0724-2 (pdf).—
ISBN 978-1-4598-0725-9 (epub)

I. Title. II. Series: Retribution (Victoria, B.C.)
PS8613.R3827E97 2015   jc813'.6   c2015-901714-9
c2015-901715-7

First published in the United States, 2015
Library of Congress Control Number: 2015935529

Summary: Stealing cars to get by and pay her debts, Raven excels at
urban climbing and takes pride in her job—until she is forced to take sides and
bring down a car-theft ring in this fast-paced entry in the Retribution trilogy.

*Orca Book Publishers is dedicated to preserving the environment and has
printed this book on Forest Stewardship Council® certified paper.*

Orca Book Publishers gratefully acknowledges the support for its publishing
programs provided by the following agencies: the Government of Canada
through the Canada Book Fund and the Canada Council for the Arts,
and the Province of British Columbia through the BC Arts Council
and the Book Publishing Tax Credit.

Cover image by iStock.com
Author photo by Curtis Comeau

ORCA BOOK PUBLISHERS
www.orcabook.com

Printed and bound in Canada.

18 17 16 15 • 4 3 2 1

To those afraid of heights
but who still make the climb.

ONE

The trouble with most people? They never look up.

They keep their eyes dead ahead, fixated as they march forward and go about getting the day done. And, like ants, they don't notice that the darkness creeping over them isn't just another storm cloud. It's a freaking shoe. No. It's a steel-toed boot on the foot of some beer-guzzling, asbestos-lunged construction worker, and the thing is going to stomp their lights out.

I thought I wasn't most people.

Guess I was wrong.

I shifted my grip on the crumbled concrete, the pull of my weight stretching the tendons in my fingers like the string on a crossbow, threatening to snap. Toes digging into the brick, I managed to snag an edge and relieve some of the pressure. I'd completed this route more times than I could count, and that was the problem. I'd been using this building for training for weeks, its brick façade perfect for an easy climb. But I'd become complacent. Forgotten my own rule. Keep your eyes on the prize.

Just like those dead-ahead ants I promised myself I'd never be.

If I had simply looked up while I'd made the climb, I would have noticed that the awning I'd decided to rest my feet on was missing a bolt, or had rusted out, or whatever made the metal bar pop from under me. Leaving me dangling by my fingertips far above a major street.

Not that any of the late-night pub crawlers noticed, too drunk to do more than put a foot in front of the other as they shuffled from one watering hole to the next.

But I'd been on automatic, not focused on where I was going and far too worried about the guy steadily climbing after me. He'd watched as the bar that had been under my feet made its clattering descent, missing his shoulder by a hair's breadth, then gone right back to picking his way up the face of the old theater.

Stubborn.

Well, so was I.

A gust of cool night air had strands of my hair dancing before my eyes. Escapees from the confines of my ponytail. I probably should cut it once and for all, but it was my claim to fame, the long, layered black hair that inspired my name, Raven. My mother used to say my perpetually messy locks looked like the ruffled tail feathers of the large black birds.

Funny, I could hear that raspy tone she had from smoking and screaming too much, but I couldn't quite picture her face. I shook my head, clearing both my mind and my vision as I climbed, springing off my perch to snag the next handhold. Where memory failed, muscle and sinew served. Handhold, foothold, reach and handhold, foothold. Motion, thought and breath in sync, I made quick work of the climb.

I scrambled over the foot-wide ledge and dropped about three feet to the roof. The red glow from the flickering marquee provided enough light for a quick scan of the perimeter. Rusted vent pipes erupted from the surface. Cracks filled with tar clawed the patchwork concrete like long black, twisted nails. Other than the cooing presence of a few pigeons, I was alone.

For the moment.

I backed away from the ledge. Waiting.

Seconds later a dark form crept over the ledge. Breath siphoned from my lungs. He'd made it. I let our gazes clash briefly, then spun on my heel and bolted across the roof. The grinding scratches of my shoes sliced through the silence as I slipped across crumbling concrete. The ledge drew closer. So did the pounding of feet behind me. I stumbled once, straightened and shifted my weight just in time. I launched forward like a circus performer gone mad, hurtling through the air. I flat-palmed the lip of the ledge and pushed off, vaulting into the night.

A dizzying blur of headlights in the distance as I crossed the seven-foot expanse over the alley. The pull of the earth, desperate to bring me down to the ground. Chin to chest, my body automatically tucked in on itself as I landed on the roof of the next building in a fluid roll, momentum driving me to my feet. I stood still. Watched as the guy neared the ledge on the building I'd just vacated. Would he make the jump?

His arms and legs pumped like mad. He just might do it.

But no.

At the last second, the guy slammed into the ledge. Instead of using it as leverage, he struck with full force, coming to a complete and utter stop with all the grace of a five-year-old using the ice-rink boards as an emergency brake. The impact had him crumbling backward.

A growl of frustration echoed across the expanse.

I threw back my head and laughed. "Maybe next time, kid."

From this angle, I could only see the top of his head as he sat there, unmoving. Maybe he'd landed harder than I thought. I frowned. "Supersize?" Named for his larger-than-life personality and not his stature—which qualified as short at best—I knew a show of concern would only make him mad. Still..."You all right?" A stream of swearwords had me smiling. "I'll take that as a yes."

Supersize struggled to his feet and approached the ledge. "So close."

He stared down at the alley below. "I almost made the jump."

"*Almost* will get you killed. You were right to bail—you waited too long to get airborne." I fired him a grin. "You weren't the only one who screwed up. I was so keen on watching you, I didn't verify my foothold with that awning. Learn from me, young Skywalker. Look before you leap."

He laughed. "You're so full of clichéd wisdom, oh ancient one."

The gibe about my upcoming birthday went unchallenged as I sauntered to the edge of the roof and swung a leg over.

"Quit trying to tick me off," I said. "I'm your ride home, remember?" Fingers locked onto the ledge, I found the first foothold and let gravity take me down until my vision barely cleared the lip. A soft, red glow backlit the kid. He was small. And so young. Still, he was older than I'd been when I started working for Diesel, back when my boss was just another car jockey. What a difference the years had made for both of us. I wasn't the same lost little girl, and Diesel was so far from the easygoing stoner who'd recruited me, he was barely recognizable. And increasingly unpredictable.

He'd said he'd let me go. That I'd done my time, served him well, and that once I turned sixteen I had a choice. Stay, or leave with his blessing. I was seriously torn. He'd taken me in when my parents had all but abandoned me for their one true love: meth. He was all the family I knew. He had given me the tools I needed to survive—I owed him my life. How could I leave when I owed him everything?

Still, there was no denying that he'd changed. And I had to admit that I was tempted to finally put my escape plan into action. That I dreamed of another life. Wondered what I could be if I had a shot at something different. And the opportunity might be at hand.

But cutting loose wasn't as easy as it sounded—and not just because I was torn. I had to train my replacement before I could leave. Diesel had grown accustomed to my unusual skill set. It was my job to scale the tallest, most exclusive, most secure parkades and give the others access from the inside. What I did—the strength, speed and sheer guts involved—had taken me years to develop. Diesel had given me mere weeks to get the kid up to speed.

"Be at the car in five or I'm leaving without you." I left my protégé to make his own descent.

Not bad for a first attempt, but not great either. I'd have to report it as I saw it, no matter the consequences. The kid was cautious. That wasn't a problem. This was dangerous work, and it paid to take your time, to have a solid game plan. We climbed without ropes, chalk or any of the usual safety gear, leaving no physical evidence behind for the cops to trace. What concerned me most was that

Supersize lacked confidence. I could get him there—a few minor successes should build him up enough—but I needed additional time.

More than I had. There were others on the team who could climb a few stories, but no one willing to go as high as I could. Supersize was my last shot. He'd showed such promise, but there was more to this job than just scaling walls. You had to be comfortable crawling all over them, jumping from rooftop to rooftop and taking controlled risks.

So far Supersize hadn't been able to push beyond his self-doubt. He was overthinking. Freaking himself out at the last minute.

My chest tightened. My breathing became strained, but not from the demands of the climb.

Diesel would not be pleased.

TWO

An hour later I pulled into the warehouse's rear bay doors and killed the engine. Through the windshield I noted the familiar two-story industrial layout with its open-beam ceiling, long row of blacked windows, and rusted metal columns.

"Thank you for a wonderful evening," Supersize said, speaking as low as his not-quite-broken voice would allow, then leaning in for a kiss like some dude from an online dating commercial. I let him get close. Let him think it was going to happen.

Then, laughing, I palmed his whole face. "Ugh. *Please.*" I twisted his head so his lips puckered into the air.

"Worth a shot." He grinned and slipped out of the car, heading toward what we jokingly called "the dorm," where he'd probably fall into an exhausted sleep. I pretended not to notice his limp. Guys and their egos and all that. His had already taken a beating.

I climbed out of the driver's seat and slammed the door.

"What is this crap?" I heard someone say. Disgust dripped from every word. To a member of a crew responsible for breaking into the city's fanciest parkades to access the expensive vehicles within, the car I'd brought to the warehouse that night was subpar to say the least.

"Come on, Link." I smiled up at the unibrow who'd come to stand at my side. Six four and bearing an uncanny resemblance to a textbook Neanderthal, The Weakest Link, or Link for short, was one of the best guys working chop. "It's not so bad."

We both examined the Honda Civic hatchback. The industrial lighting wasn't kind. Rusted wheel wells. Bondo patches. Not my best work. Usually my hauls were higher-end vehicles, 4x4s, SUVs or sedans that'd be sent to the dock and loaded into shipping containers. But tonight I'd hotwired whatever was around to give Supersize a taste of the adventure.

Didn't tell him the rush is a lot like chewing gum—intense at first, but all too soon your jaw is working clay.

"I'll make it up to you," I said, flashing Link a smile.

He wagged a finger at me. "Now quit that. I'm not falling for those come-and-get-me eyes, and long lashes…"

"*Come-and-get-me eyes*?" I smirked, impressed. "Really?"

Link flushed and backed away a few paces. "Get out of here, Raven. Some of us have work to do."

Laughing, I spun on my heel and left him to it. I took the stairs to Diesel's second-floor office two at a time. Years ago the warehouse had served as a bottle actory, and then it was abandoned. Most industrial buildings were snapped up by developers and turned into condos, but Diesel had lucked out. Thanks to his unnamed connection in the city zoning department, no one had ever come sniffing around. If they had, they wouldn't have seen much beyond the crumbling facade of the exterior walls and boarded windows.

The inside was another story.

Two levels of genius. The lower level had bays to temporarily store stolen cars and a chop station for dismantling. The upper floor was Diesel's "central command" and an entire converted wing of small rooms that housed those on the team who had no other place to go. The warehouse was a refuge.

We took care of each other. When I'd told the kid I was taking him home, I meant it.

For some of us, this place was the only home we knew.

As I approached Diesel's office, voices rose angrily over the clatter and squeal of power tools. My footsteps slowed. If Diesel was having words with someone, I'd have to bide my time and wait. Diesel had become the king of his very own empire. But it hadn't come easy. Every success seemed to set him more on edge. The better he did, the higher his expectations for next time. His ring was one of many; if he failed to meet demand, his clients would go elsewhere.

The constant pressure was getting to him.

Changing him.

The sound of a fist meeting a face came through the walls loud and clear. I flinched as if I'd been hit.

"When I say we need more, I mean it." Diesel's voice was thick with rage. "I better give him another demonstration—I'm not sure he heard me over his crying."

My stomach rolled. This was our home, but it no longer felt like a safe haven.

The office door opened, and one of the older boys was shoved out. He staggered on his feet, cupping a hand over his bleeding nose. Bruising already building under his eyes.

I leaped forward, trying to help, but he shoved me against the railing and bolted down the stairs.

Catching my breath, I gripped the railing and shook off my anger. I knew it wasn't right that Diesel was getting physical with some of the boys, roughing them up more and more when things didn't go as planned. But he still kept us fed, with a roof over our heads, and saved all of us from the streets.

This was just a temporary thing, I told myself. He'd be back to normal once the pressure was off. We owed him our loyalty, our lives. Below, I had a clear view of the chop crew already stripping the hatchback I'd stolen of its license plate and the cartoon-family decals on the rear window. I gripped the railing, tremors of fear settling in my bones. I wasn't looking forward to telling Diesel the kid needed more time.

The voices grew louder.

"I don't care what Bowdin said." Diesel's usually smooth voice had serated teeth and cut through the glass and wood, making it impossible to do anything but eavesdrop. "Or Livingston, or Darwell. Those guys strut around in business suits, barking out orders at their cell phones and thinking they're above me. I'm the one at ground zero."

"But distribution is what this business is all about. Without them—" began Wheels, Diesel's second in command, only to be cut off by a hiss of anger.

"Don't tell me what I already know," Diesel said. "They demand. We supply. Some schmuck transports. That's the order of things. Period. When the suits start dipping their noses in, things go wrong. Businessmen and corrupt government officials. What do they know about this life except how much money we make them? I won't have them sniffing around my shop, telling me how to increase production or questioning how I handle things."

Tension crawled up my spine. Diesel was already riled up. Screw waiting. I just wanted the badness over with. I slipped by the window to stand before the office door, my fist hovering, waiting for the right moment to knock.

"We have to stay one step ahead of the competition," Diesel was saying. "Gotta keep our heads straight. If I find out you've been using again, you're history."

That was one thing I'd always respected about Diesel. He might be running a car-theft ring and chop shop, but it was a drug-free working environment. A rare thing in this industry. If anyone in the warehouse used, they'd be tossed back out on the streets. If help was needed, it was freely given, but there were no second chances. Diesel had gone through rehab and changed his life. They say there's nothing worse than an ex-smoker, and that was Diesel exactly. Zero tolerance.

Most of the kids he took in were like m̸
orphaned by meth. I was just the first to
benefit from Diesel's reformed ways.

He'd always had a soft spot for me.

But lately even I'd been on the wrong
side of Diesel's machete-sharp temper.

I swallowed back the unease scaling
my throat and rapped my knuckles on the
door. Twice. Hard.

The door swung open. Wheels stormed
past me, his short, wide, bodybuilder's
form filling the narrow walkway, muscles
straining under his white wife-beater shirt.

"Ah, Raven, you're like a breath of
night air." Diesel stepped from behind his
desk and waved me inside. No sign of the
beating he'd doled out or the anger he'd
been spewing at Wheels in the wide smile
he offered. "How did it go with the boy?
What's his name again? Supersize?"

"Not how I'd hoped." I let out a breath.
"He picks things up. Fast. He's strong.
Smart."

"I feel a *but* coming."

"If I could just have a few more weeks."

"You do. There are exactly three weeks from now until your sixteenth birthday."

I sighed. "A few *more.*"

"Raven." Diesel's smile faded. "I'm afraid that's not part of our deal. Either the boy is ready to assume your duties, and you are free to leave the warehouse if you so wish, or he's not, and you stay and life continues as it has always done while you continue to prepare him for future assignments." He frowned. "Haven't you been training nonstop? Almost to the point of neglecting your studies? And school being so very important to you."

Only Diesel could sound concerned and condescending at once. "Yes, but Supersize needs a few test drives under his belt. Easy climbs to build his confidence. He's okay with scaling, but jumps, the descent..." I shook my head. "A few more weeks, then maybe..."

Diesel cleared his throat, stood tall and met my gaze with a level stare. "We have a rush order. It just came in. I need all hands on deck to make this happen. I had hoped to have you both leading separate teams."

Immediately, I held up a hand. "No way." My words a growl. At the dark scowl that formed on Diesel's face, I struggled to keep my tone civil. Diesel had to understand that Supersize couldn't be put out in the field. "The kid choked on a jump tonight. He needs a few days in the gym, hooked up to the ropes. A little reinforcing of the basics."

Diesel took a deep breath, and the redness began to fade from his jawline. "He's your apprentice, Raven. I'll let this be your call. If he's not ready for a solo mission, he's not ready."

I wasn't quite convinced. "Promise me you won't put him out there until I say so." If there was one thing I could count on, it was Diesel's word.

"If you say so."

With that, our discussion ended.

It was only later that I realized he never promised me a thing.

THREE

It was bad enough that everyone in Advanced English class turned to stare at me when Mr. Nicholson dramatically announced the title of his poem of the day, "Caged Bird," by Maya Angelou.

To have him recite the thing while standing in front of my desk was an unjustified punishment. Hadn't I made it to class—on time—every day for the last month? Thankfully, the poem was on the shorter side of eternal torment.

As the last word of the poem echoed in the pin-drop silence, I had to admit, Nicholson could work a crowd. He bowed at the burst of applause. "Why, thank you, students." He started for the front of the class, shooting me a grin over his shoulder. "Forgive me, dear Raven, I couldn't resist."

Well, at least he hadn't recited Poe.

Again.

I hunched over my desk, letting my hair slip over my shoulders and shield my face from view. Blocking out the world and everyone in it.

Except for the guy up one row to my left.

He'd shifted to sit sideways in his seat as soon as Nicholson started in with the poem, resting a muscular arm along the back of his chair. Black hoodie molded to his shoulders like form-fitting armor. Dark eyes steady on mine until the shrill bell rang and the girl in front of me stood to leave, severing our contact sharply, like a knife between the ribs.

I bolted from the room. Once in the hallway, I sucked in a deep breath. Give me a dangerous late-night solo climb in the rain, and I'd be solid as a rock. But one long look from Emmett Daniels and I lost my nerve.

Stupid high-school-girl fantasies. Where was my head? I had more important things to stress about than getting the attention of some guy. With a bit of a rebel vibe. And strong hands.

"Raven, hold up."

And a voice that could have melted the iceberg that sank the *Titanic*. Low and gravelly and warm all at once. I felt myself slipping under the waves.

This was tragic, all right.

Kids flooded the hallway, and I took advantage of the crush of bodies to weave through the crowd, leaving Emmett looking this way and that, trying to find me in the commotion.

Our paths didn't cross again until History in last block. By then I had a plan. A surefire way to nix Emmett's interest and save us both some heartache. Hanging out with guys, flirting and keeping it light, was one thing. But with Emmett things felt different. Heavy. Intense.

I had no business getting involved with a guy like that.

One who mattered.

Emmett Daniels was everything I'd ever wanted.

But his father was a cop.

A freaking *cop*.

When Emmett strode into class, his gaze quickly finding me, eyes narrowing with frustration and maybe a bit of hurt, I thought I was prepared for the fallout.

Instead, my stomach twisted with regret.

Ian Hudson, golden boy of the lacrosse team, seemed to sense my unease as I perched on his knees. The arm he'd thrown across my narrow waist tightened, and he nuzzled my ear. "Where have you been all my life?" His stage whisper drew laughs from the other students who filed into class, watching our antics with either amused or envious stares.

Except for Emmett. Jaw clenched, he turned away from us and made for the back of the room.

"Ladies and gentlemen." Mrs. Sennway cleared her throat. "Let's get started, shall we?" She noticed my unusual seating arrangement and raised a brow. "If everyone could take their seats, we'll begin with some current events."

The class groaned as Sennway held up a newspaper clipping.

As she read the article aloud, I tried to leave Ian's lap gracefully, but he made a show of holding me in place. In case Emmett was watching, I struggled to keep a sultry smile on my lips, all the while mentally slapping Ian upside the head.

"Let me go, Ian." I singsonged the words just loud enough for him to hear.

"Make me." He chuckled under his breath.

Well, he'd asked for it.

I grabbed his middle finger and reefed it backward. His knuckle popped, and with a pained yelp he set me free.

I slipped into an empty desk, unable to resist a quick glance at Emmett. He seemed to find Sennway's article fascinating. Wow. Maybe that had really done it. Emmett had finally gotten the hint I wasn't interested. I focused on Sennway and ignored the weird tripping of my heart. What was she saying? Something about rituals. A sense of belonging. Perpetuating mystery. Ah…I got it. The article compared the origins of secret societies with youth gangs.

Both play on an individual's desire to belong, to have a sense of power, and to benefit from the group's protection.

I swallowed back a curse. They made it sound so romantic. I thought of Diesel and the constant threats he faced, the demands for more product, more money, more kids to work the ring. The ones before me who'd aged out. Where had they really ended up? In college,

like I hoped I would in a few months?
Or in jail?

Or dead?

The rest of the class passed in a haze.
When the bell rang, I gathered up my
things. Emmett dropped a torn piece of
paper on my desk, then stalked down the
aisle and out the door.

I stared down at the note he'd written.

My heart triple-timed.

What's YOUR secret?

FOUR

I bolted from the school. I needed to get away from Emmett's looming presence and the niggling urge to answer his question. To share my secrets. To be honest with a guy for once in my life and see what would happen.

Hopping a bus, I shuffled to the rear exit and leaned my back against the metal bar at the edge of the narrow stairway. Music screamed in my earbuds as downtown Vancouver slipped by.

Here's the thing. I was attending Laurier Secondary under a false last name and a sob story about moving in with my nonexistent cousin after my parents "died."

The only reason the school had let me in without many questions? My grades. Now, I'm no genius or anything. Let's just say my marks were good enough to boost any school's achievement rankings.

I had mad climbing, coordination and gymnastic skills but pretended to be allergic to my own sweat in gym class to avoid being asked to join any sports teams. And while other kids were working at the Cineplex, doling out popcorn and sodas, my part-time job was scaling buildings and stealing cars.

Then there was the big daddy of all secrets, which I'd kept from Diesel for over a year. I didn't spend my share of our take on clothes like he thought I did—I just shopped at consignment stores, scooping up designer labels at bargain-bin prices so he'd think I frittered my money away. As if a stellar wardrobe was more important than sheer survival. No, I'd done the impossible. Put one over on Diesel and invested in my very own personal escape plan.

I don't know how long I rode that bus, but I'd made it through my playlist several times. The afternoon sun had faded to dusk. Seeing a few familiar landmarks, I reached up and pulled the cord. Soon the bus eased to a stop, and then I was striding smoothly down the street, keen to reach my destination.

And there it was. My secret, my escape plan. A fully functional, if slightly weathered, forty-foot fishing trawler turned liveaboard, moored in a marina steps from downtown Vancouver.

So Emmett's note about my secret simply had me asking, Which freaking one?

Still, none of this—the note, his attempts to get me to talk with him— would have happened if I had kept focused on my goal. My mission to blend, to be just another girl on the fringe of all things. Noticed, perhaps, but not sought out. Not needed by anyone. Or wanted.

Until Emmett and that weirdly addictive kiss in the school library. Right there in the stacks between the automotive-repair manuals and the encyclopedias. Up to then, Emmett and I had been skirting around each other, testing boundaries. But in those few amazing seconds, the world had shifted under my feet.

No matter how hard I tried to get back to where I was before the kiss, Emmett was determined to keep me off-kilter. Not good. Especially when I needed my head in the game. Diesel was counting on me.

And so was Supersize.

All these conflicting emotions made my muscles twitch. I needed some distance, some perspective. I needed to move. To work off some tension. In seconds I was halfway up the brick facade of the nearest three-story building, a smile of exhilaration on my lips.

From here all my worries seemed smaller. So small they could be tucked away in my pocket and forgotten, like empty candy wrappers that would someday just slip away unnoticed. Clouds drifted high above buildings, cars, and people scurrying down sidewalks. Ginormous cotton balls in a silent march to the sea. Boats moored along the marina swayed with the breeze and the waves kicked up by a passing ferry. Bonaparte's gulls, gray-and-white bodies with dark masked faces, swooped low, buzzing and cawing into the wind. The bandits of the skies.

How I envied them their ability to soar above the world and all its madness. All the lies, fights and epic tragedies. The guys like Diesel, in over their heads and sinking fast. Kids like me, trapped in a life we didn't ask for but were making the most of. We were the same, all of us, as the bird in the poem Nicholson had recited. Caged in the what-ifs and if-onlys of our lives, unable to do more than sing about freedom.

I made it to the roof and let out a breath. Huh, wouldn't Nicholson be thrilled to know he had me getting all lofty and philosophical? Time to go before I lost complete touch with reality.

How to get down? Back the way I came or...no...the fire-escape ladder would do just fine. Faster and more fun.

I climbed over the wall and stepped down onto the second rung. I pulled the cuffs of my hoodie to cover my palms, cupped the outside of the railing with the inside arch of my cross trainers and let myself slide down the rest of the way. My descent—a blur of speed, but light and controlled. A foot from the ground, I pushed off the rail and landed. Feet planted firmly, bent knees absorbing the impact.

The shocked face of a guy about Supersize's age filled my vision. Bony shoulders, thin frame. He'd been limping along, but my dramatic entrance on the sidewalk made him come to a full stop.

"Having fun?" he asked. His voice surprisingly high-pitched.

"Time of my life." I paused, taking in the guy's fine features, the flash of something in his dark eyes. Panic? Desperation? Charged from the climb but craving more action, I spun on my heel and started down the sidewalk in a light jog. Whatever his trouble, I had enough of my own. Besides, he looked like he'd live to fight the good fight yet another day.

Not everyone was so lucky.

A few minutes later I hopped onto the deck of *Big Daddy*—AKA my secret hideaway that could someday be a lifesaving getaway—my own houseboat. I turned on the sink faucet and poured a steady stream of water into a small potted plant I'd named Charlie. I had a thing about that plant. Diesel was allergic to pets and plants alike. This little green mass with its bright yellow blooms was the only living thing I'd been able to care for and call my own. The boat was my ticket to freedom. If things got too hairy with Diesel, I'd simply untie the lines and go.

In theory.

But there were more than a few ropes holding me to Diesel. He'd taken me off the streets. Given me a roof over my head and a job to do, and surrounded me with people I considered family. I wouldn't leave him in the lurch. Not when there was a price on his head if he didn't keep the suits happy. And if Supersize wasn't ready to take on my usual duties, I'd have to stay.

Screw Sennway and her dinner-by-five, in-bed-by-nine high-school-teacher view of why kids stay in gangs. This wasn't just looking for a place to belong. This was family. And family was everything—especially when you didn't have one of your own.

Or you did.

But they chose drugs over you long ago.

FIVE

Later that night I was in the thick of it with my "family," but I wasn't feeling the love. In fact, I was feeling a lot like a glorified evil-crime nanny. One whose charges were being troublesome because they were actually behaving properly.

We didn't need proper. We needed more product. Diesel had sent two teams out, pitting us against each other in a "bit of friendly competition"—winners would have two nights of freedom. Kat was heading up the other team, and I had to admit Diesel's plan was working.

I wanted to win. I could do a lot in two nights of no reporting back to the shop.

Make sure my boat was stocked with supplies. Wrap my head around what I was going to do about Emmett.

But winning meant bringing in the best haul. My crew had been scouting the dark streets of a run-down residential area on the edge of the city center, and so far we hadn't bagged a single set of wheels.

"What is wrong with you guys?" I placed my hands on my hips. "You heard Diesel. Our average three cars a night isn't enough. Not anymore. Anything with a decent engine is a target at this point. And you four"—I nodded to Supersize and the three guys standing around him—"will stick to the houses. Get in, grab what you can, get out."

"This is bull." Supersize hunched his shoulders. "I should be shadowing you, not back on break-ins."

I sighed. We'd been over this already. "Look, you started with houses. It's what you're best at"—I spoke over Supersize's mulish expression—"right *now*. You wanted to take on some leadership roles, young man." I grinned. "Here's your chance to show your boys how it's done." Turning to face the others, I gave the order to move. "All right, let's do this."

Supersize grudgingly led his crew into the night, while the three kids I'd pegged for car duty slipped off in different directions. In seconds we'd fanned out over the entire sleepy neighborhood like a pack of hungry coyotes.

Around the corner, a cul-de-sac beckoned. I'd sidled up to a purple PT Cruiser when a flash of movement caught my eye. Which one of my crew was being that obvious? I crept closer to get a better look. The kid hovered under a floodlight beaming down from a garage door.

Deer in the headlights.

Wait a minute. That wasn't anyone from the warehouse. It was the kid I'd almost flattened on the sidewalk earlier in the day. The one who looked like trouble was his only friend. I shook my head.

This wasn't going to end well. He strode right up the sidewalk to the front door and pulled out…was that some kind of lockpick? Using my well-earned stealth, I moved across the lawn and was at his back in a heartbeat.

"Are you totally stupid?" I asked.

The guy whirled around. I squinted down at him—hard. No way. He wasn't a he; he was a *she*. Long hair had come loose from under the girl's baseball cap. I was surprised I'd fallen for such an obvious ploy, but then, simple was sometimes most effective.

"What the—how did you get here?"

"With my feet, newb."

"An urban climber walking? Shouldn't you be swinging from a web?"

"That's Spider-Man."

"This can't be a coincidence." She folded her arms across her chest. "Are you following me? What do you want?"

"Watching grass grow would be more interesting than following you. Anyway, don't be stupid. It's a prime neighbor-hood. Why wouldn't we both end up here? It's got choice pickings."

"Fine. Go away."

"What are you doing?"

"Setting up for a game of checkers. What does it look like?"

"Looks like you're getting ready to get arrested for attempted B and E." I paused. "That's breaking and entering."

"Yeah, I managed to puzzle that one out."

"So? What's going on?"

"None of your business."

"It is if you get us caught." I came up the steps.

"Us?" The girl looked around. "You have a team looting the houses here?"

Well, she had a brain that worked part of the time at least. "Did you even check to see if the house is alarmed?"

"I'm not an idiot."

"You are if you're breaking in through the front door."

"Thanks for the tip, but you notice the trees cover me. Go away." She pushed past me, stepped down the stairs and headed to the back door.

"You don't have any bags. No car."

"No wonder you're a climber. Talk about eagle eyes."

"Spotted your sorry attempt to play cat burglar from a hundred feet, didn't I?"

She didn't say anything.

I sighed. "I'll keep watch."

"Why?"

"'Cause if I don't, you'll ruin the neighborhood for the rest of us. I'll give you a signal if anyone comes your way."

"What's the signal?"

"Me screaming, 'Run!'"

That made her laugh. "Fair enough."

We got to the back, and it took her ten seconds to open the door. "See?"

I shrugged. Yeah, she'd gotten in, but her technique was sloppy. "I'm beside myself, I'm so impressed."

We stepped into the quiet house. The girl totally ignored the flat-screen, the surround sound. She just kept scanning. This wasn't a random job. She knew what she was after.

"You're lucky they don't have an alarm system," I said. My cell phone vibrated in my pocket. Members of my team were moving out. "Hey!" I prompted. "You sightseeing or shopping?"

"Stay here. Watch the door." The girl pulled out a flashlight and strode into the kitchen. She waved the thing around enough to bring on a seizure. Why did I always take on the underdogs? Then she aimed the beam at the living room.

"Get what you need," I said through my teeth, "and get out."

She jumped at the sound of my voice. "I thought you were keeping watch."

"You seem like you need supervision." I moved to the fridge and opened the door. "Geez. There are enough meds in here to start a pharmacy." I leaned in and read the name on a prescription label. "Dollie Sharma."

"Close the door—you're letting out the light."

"I'm hungry." I pulled a soda from the door. "And thirsty."

"Got it." The girl stuffed a laptop into her bag as she bolted for the kitchen door.

"All that for a laptop?" I followed.

"It's what's inside that counts."

"According to you and Big Bird."

"Thanks for your help—if I can call it that…"

"Raven. My name's Raven. And you can call it whatever you want," I said as I closed the refrigerator door. "Just be smarter next time." I stopped and glanced around the kitchen. Going to a pad of paper, I scribbled my number, then handed it to her.

She took the paper. "Yeah. Right."

We walked to the front of the house. I took off, heading to Salter Street to meet up with the crew.

SIX

Diesel rode us hard the next night, and then on Friday—the best night for car nabbing because the masses were out clubbing and taking cabs so they could get completely wasted—he upped the stakes. He sent two groups of us out on a mission to up his tally. The challenge? Ten vehicles in a single night. Normally, that would be divided equally, five per team. But he'd made Supersize the other team leader.

Even though I had said he wasn't ready.

All of this meant I intended my team to do the bulk of the heavy lifting and score at least seven rides so Supersize wouldn't feel as much pressure. I'd also ranted at him before we left the warehouse. "My team takes the high ground. Don't climb more than two stories. You may think you're ready for more, but I promise you, when your blood is pumping and the job is live, sometimes you take risks. Things go south, and they always do, you just react instead of sticking to the plan. Those are rookie mistakes that can get you in serious trouble." Supersize grinned up at me. "Why are you smiling?" I narrowed my eyes, hoping I looked as fierce as I felt at that moment. "Do you see me smiling? This isn't a joke."

"If you could see how hot you look right now…"

I made a face. "Seriously? You're such a freaking boy." I shoved the laughing Supersize out of my way and gathered the rest of my team.

We would keep in contact via text.

* * *

Two hours later, and so far so good. Each team had six bodies. One trailing on lookout, one scouting ahead for potential targets on street level, and four doing the actual thefts. This involved breaking into the vehicles and driving them back to the warehouse. Supersize's crew had two cars bagged to our four. I hoped this last parkade would do the trick.

Once I got in, I'd use one of the parked vehicles' automatic remotes to open the bay doors and establish access for the others waiting on the ground.

I focused on the goal, slipping easily into the zone. The scuff of my shoes on the wall and the rasp of my breath beat in time with the distant thrum of late-night traffic and the pounding of my heart. Growing louder in my ears by the second.

This had to be quick. It had to go smoothly.

I reached for the next handhold, and as my fingers scraped along the rough brick wall, I was thankful for the calluses that had built up on my fingertips. Sixty feet below, my team watched my progress from the ground, waiting for me to gain access from the roof and open the door from the inside, bypassing the security system. A parkade like this had no internal alarms, relying entirely on its imposing height and a token number of cameras at the entrance.

The sound of sirens cut through the night, drifting to my ears from far below. The rhythmic screams drew closer.

Better get a move on.

The pounding of my heart grew louder. Almost there. I glanced at the roof edge, just a few feet farther up, only to be blasted by a brilliant white light. Blinded, I froze in place, clung to the wall and turned my head away from the light. Blinked away a serious case of sundogs.

Only, at two in the morning, it wasn't the sun beaming down into the night, and it wasn't my heart I'd been hearing, but a police helicopter. The searchlight was aimed at the street below.

Son of a...

Shuffling along sideways, I tucked my body into a hollow gap in the facade near an air vent. Just wide enough for me to slip into and hide in the shadows.

My brain raced. The sirens. The chopper. The cops were hunting someone down. Someone close. I hoped it wasn't Supersize. I had to get topside so I could call and see if he and his crew were all right. If I was lucky, the cops would just scan the ground for their suspect and not even spare a glance at the sides of buildings.

By now, everyone from my crew on the ground would have scattered. All part of the training Diesel so kindly provided. At the first sign of the cops, everyone knew the drill.

Don't get caught, even if it means leaving someone behind. How was that for one big happy crime family?

Still, we all understood the logic. One member of the ring getting caught was nothing, easily glossed over as a botched first attempt by a rookie car thief acting alone. That's how the cops Diesel had on the inside would handle it. But two or more hogtied and brought in? Now that was trouble. That led to Diesel's cops having to report to higher-ups and being unable to contain the damage. We were talking a special investigation team.

Then the suits would really lose their profit-loving minds.

And the infinitely scary side of Diesel would be out in full force.

The spotlight zigzagged over the streets below, working away from my location. I let out a breath. That was close. Too close. I shifted out of the gap and reached the roof in record time. Once over the edge, I plunked down on the concrete, pressing my back against the perimeter wall and keeping myself small in case the chopper returned.

I fired a quick text, the one Supersize and I had established as a warning to bail on whatever job we'd been assigned: **Get home now or you're grounded for life.** I waited five minutes. He should have replied by then if all was well.

My stomach knotted with dread as I bolted for the rooftop door and entered the parkade. I hotwired the first set of wheels I saw and got out to the street. None of my crew waited in the shadows, which wasn't unexpected. They'd have scattered when they saw the chopper. But the sirens in the distance, the chopper… something had gone down, and whatever it was, it was close. I knew in my heart it had to do with Supersize. I rushed for the warehouse, skidding around corners and running red lights. Zero thoughts of being stealthy or playing it safe.

I had the steering wheel in a death grip, but my hands still trembled in shock.

"Please be okay, please…" A plea, a prayer I repeated over and over again, but deep down I knew they were just words.

Powerless. Helpless.

Like me.

I peeled into the warehouse, sending the chop-shop guys off in all directions. I bolted from the SUV I'd stolen, leaving the driver's door wide open and the engine running. Link was waiting, arms folded across his chest.

"Is everyone back?" I asked, spinning in a slow circle.

"Yeah, sure." Link popped the hood of the SUV, and his voice grew muffled. "Your crew's all accounted for." Besides the usual grease monkeys, kids from my team gathered around, showing off their rides. Faces glowing. No hint of drama. Just the rush of a job well done and coming out on top of a close call.

Still, my gut told me the ax was about to fall.

"*My crew,*" I echoed. "What about Supersize and his team?"

Link peeked out from under the hood. He leveled his gaze on mine. "No sign of them yet." The tension in his voice betrayed his concern. "Radio silence too."

At least I wasn't the only one stressing about Supersize not having checked in. I glanced up at Diesel's office. Blinds down. No lights. Figured. "When will he be back?"

Link shrugged. "Your guess is as good as mine. The boss hasn't been exactly forthcoming lately."

"Hey, Link," one of the guys working the bay doors called out. "What do you make of this?" Link and I stared at the small monitor mounted on the wall, displaying video from the security cameras. Yeah, a car-theft ring with security. I was aware of the irony.

But Diesel liked to know what was coming his way.

And from the look of the five kids at the doors, some with expressions of absolute blankness, what was coming wasn't anything good. They'd shut down.

"Open her up. Up. Up." Link waved his arms at the doors. "Get them inside." The clanging metal lifted, and the other team stumbled across the threshold.

Everyone but Supersize.

Kat, one of the smaller girls, who'd been around almost as long as I had, met my gaze and slowly shook her head. She didn't have to say anything.

I already knew he was gone.

* * *

When Diesel finally returned for the night, he wanted all the gory details. I suffered through Kat's retelling of the events leading up to Supersize's death. How he'd insisted on climbing one of the newly constructed car parks. The ones with all the reflective glass and few hand- and footholds. Buildings even *I* avoided.

Kat and the rest of his team had waited below. They debated calling me, but no one did.

About halfway up, Supersize lost his grip. Fell thirty feet.

"We didn't believe it at first. Thought he'd be able to grab on. But he just slid down the glass. We could hear him screaming," Kat choked out.

I closed my eyes, imagining it. The panic, the terror, as he scratched at the unforgiving glass. His own reflection screaming back at him.

"He landed on one of those airport-limo rides," she continued. "Set the alarm off. There were a bunch of people on the street. They filed out of the bars to see what was going on. Someone must have called 9-1-1. When they heard the sirens, the rest of the team took off, but I hung around until the chopper showed." She sucked in a shaky breath. "They lit him up for a long time before moving on. Once I saw he was really dead, I left."

There was a long moment of silence.

"Is there anything I need to worry about?" Diesel asked.

"No," Kat answered, her voice firm. "I got close. He was…" Her voice broke. She shook her head and began again. "He was crushed by the impact."

"Thank you," Diesel said finally. "You may go."

Kat wrapped her arms around me in a fierce hug. Whispered into my ear, "Diesel made him do the climb. Threatened him, Raven. Said you'd never get your chance to leave the warehouse if he didn't do it."

My breath caught in my throat, and I couldn't respond. Supersize had been trying to protect me. To make sure I got my happy ending. And Diesel…he'd pay.

"I'm so sorry, Raven," Kat said in a normal tone, stepping back. "He was a good kid."

I nodded, fighting back tears. Now wasn't the time to lose it.

When the office door closed behind Kat, I stared at the floor. Diesel and his two goons talked together in low tones, giving me a moment to think. I struggled to pull myself together. The crying could wait. I stuffed all the rage, the pain and the guilt deep down so I could say what had to be said.

I owed it to Supersize.

Dead inside, I lifted my chin. "I told you he wasn't ready." Speech was difficult, my mouth dry with tension.

Diesel pursed his lips. "Yes."

"But you still gave him a team. Threw that challenge in our faces like a freaking red flag. You knew he'd do whatever it took to get your attention." I concentrated on keeping my voice even, with no betraying waver of fear.

A flush surged up Diesel's neck. His dark eyes narrowed.

Sure, I'd sassed Diesel before, but I'd never openly challenged him, and certainly not in front of witnesses.

"Now, there's where I think you have it wrong, Raven." He pushed his chair back and came out from behind his desk. His goons flanked him, making an imposing line.

Knees trembling, I fought the urge to back down and retreat a few paces. They had their height and muscle, but I had a well of anger to draw on. I stood my ground.

"I barely knew the boy." Diesel held out open hands as if to say, *Sorry, it wasn't me.* "Supersize didn't attempt to climb that building to catch *my* eye. He knew very well that his status in the ring depended on one person—his mentor."

And then I understood who Diesel was going to pin this on.

"The only person Supersize was out to impress was you." Diesel and his goons shared a look of confirmation. When he met my betrayed gaze, his expression darkened. "I know it's tough to swallow, Raven, but it's your fault the boy is dead."

SEVEN

My fault?

Was it? Diesel had used Supersize's feelings for me and his generous nature against him, but without me as motivation, Supersize wouldn't have attempted such a dangerous climb.

I dragged my feet through the halls of Laurier Secondary in a haze of grief. Everything from my looming birthday to Emmett's dark, searching looks faded to white noise. Drifting from class to class took little effort. I was on autopilot, but at least I wasn't on crash and burn.

I'd held it together so far. Mostly because of the burning rage deep in my gut, simmering under the confusion and the heavy weight of guilt. By morning, Diesel's theory of me being responsible for Supersize's death had made the rounds. I knew why he'd done it. He couldn't afford to have his decisions questioned. So he'd made me the fall guy.

But understanding his logic didn't mean it didn't sting like hell. The man I'd looked at as a father, the man I'd encouraged other kids to trust, had betrayed me. Had gotten Supersize killed. The pain was constant, like an open wound. Exposed. Raw.

And what cut even deeper? Everyone agreed with him, it seemed. It had been decided that I'd been negligent in my mentorship and Supersize had paid the price. Even Link wouldn't meet my gaze when I left for school.

I swallowed the lump of bitterness in my throat and entered my English class. I lingered just inside the entrance. Nope. Wasn't happening.

I had zero interest in sitting through another of the teacher's recitations or facing the stares of the other students as they noticed my red-rimmed eyes, raw from holding back tears.

And a tidal wave of self-doubt hit me.

Maybe it *was* my fault that Supersize had gone against every bit of advice I'd ever given him. I'd set out to protect him. But he'd gone and lost his life trying to protect me. Diesel had everyone convinced I'd gone too far. That I'd stifled Supersize's abilities. So much so that he had put his own life on the line to prove he was ready to fill my shoes. Did they really think the kid had wanted my place in the ring that badly?

Couldn't they see Diesel for what he really was?

A user. A manipulator.

Not the only family I'd ever really known.

He was a lie.

The tears came then. Uncontrollable. I was out of control. Had to get out of there.

I spun on my heel to burst through the door, hoping for a clean exit, but I slammed into a wall.

No, not a wall, but a guy's solid chest.

"Sorry," I said, pushing off lean muscle and shooting a glance upward. Stifled a curse.

Emmett's face, narrowed in concern, stared down at me. "Raven, you okay?"

"Back off." I held up a finger in warning. "I can't deal with you right now."

Emmett took a few steps backward into the hallway. "Deal with me?" he repeated. Concern shifted to frustration. "Why, what did I do?"

"You're just…always around." I waved a hand to take in the whole school in general. "You show up at all the wrong times." I sniffled, swiping a hand at my wet cheeks. "With the *looking* at me. And trying to figure me out. You're just so…

so…" I couldn't explain my reaction to Emmett—not even to myself. Words failed.

"So *what*?" Emmett stepped closer, warmth from his body seeping into mine, which was still numb with shock from all I'd been through over the last twenty-four hours. "What am I to you, Raven?"

What was he to me? A ghost of what could be? A dream I wished I'd never had? Yet there he was, pushing at me. Real. Warm.

Alive.

"This…" I grabbed him by his hoodie, pulled him down and crushed my lips against his. Our teeth crashed together, and I moaned in frustration, easing the pressure enough for our mouths to move on each other. For a heartbeat, a really awkward *thaa-thunk* of time, I was the only one doing the kissing. Before I could pull away in complete embarrassment, Emmett's lips moved under mine. Coaxing. Drawing me in. He'd changed my wild attack into something softer, deeper and way, way scarier.

Our kiss ended as a smattering of applause echoed in the hall. I buried my face in Emmett's neck. What was I thinking? That was exactly the problem. All I could do was feel. Pain. Desire. A yearning for more than I deserved.

Supersize had wanted more too. Look where it had gotten him. In a body bag at the morgue.

Diesel's orders or not, his blood was on my hands.

Ignoring the kids who'd stopped to observe our public demonstration of obsession, Emmett hugged me tightly. I savored the sensation of him all around me, then did what I had to.

I slipped from his arms. "Please, just let me go."

And, he did.

EIGHT

I spent the rest of the afternoon topside, legs dangling over the edge of Laurier Secondary's newly tarred roof, protected from view by some vents and a small alcove where the rest of the school met the gym wall. Below, the school parking lot was filled with vehicles and little else. Tucked high above the angst and issues of high school life, I came to terms with a lot of things.

Things most other kids my age couldn't even begin to imagine. There was no way to deny the truth.

The family I thought I'd had... didn't exist.

Diesel had sent Supersize on a job he knew the kid couldn't handle. All because his bosses were breathing down his neck and he needed to move more product. I finally saw Diesel clearly.

He didn't care about any of us. We were just commodities to be exploited as he saw fit. He might have saved me from life with my parents, but I'd just traded one toxic family for another.

He gave all of us the illusion of safety, of freedom, so we'd never think of running away. How many more would fall under his spell? Waste their lives making him rich?

A buzzing in my back pocket made me jump. If that was Diesel, I wasn't sure how I'd sound. Stressed out? Suspicious? Out for revenge? But it wasn't Diesel. I didn't recognize the number, but I answered anyway.

"Raven, this is you, right? The climber? It's Jo—you know, from the house the other night?"

It took a second, but then I recognize the voice. It was the guy-girl who'd needed my help breaking into a house on that quiet cul-de-sac. Well, *needed* might be too strong a word, but still, I'd made sure she hadn't done anything totally stupid.

Like get herself caught.

"Yeah, Jo, I remember." Had to appreciate the idea of a name that worked whether she was guying or girling it up.

"Good, that's good. That's great." There was a brief pause. Then Jo spoke in a rush. "I need your help. There's this guy at this school, and I need him to help me. Well, not him but his friend. He's a hacker, and I need access to…well…stuff…and…"

"Slow down, Jo. You're not making any sense." My brain hurt from trying to keep up with this one-sided conversation. "Just tell me three things: who's the mark, what's the objective, and what's in it for me."

After a moment of panicked breaths, Jo gave me the information I needed.

have to find a friend of mine. I think a corrupt cop has her. I don't know what's going to happen to her, but it can't be good. Jace Wyatt knows a hacker who can get me the information I need, and if you help me get him on my side, someday I'll return the favor."

I made some noncommittal noise. She'd kind of floored me. If moving cars was dangerous, going up against cops was suicide. Hadn't I pegged her as trouble from the beginning? This wasn't my fight. I had my own dragons to slay. Still, there was something about Jo that made me want to protect her. Like if I helped her, I'd be making up for my failure to ensure that Supersize was ready for all Diesel would throw at him.

That was it. The reason I couldn't get Supersize's death out of my head.

Guilt gnawed at me.

"I'm serious, Raven." Something in her voice made the no I was about to set free die in my throat. "I don't have anyone else to ask. But I swear to you, I have to find Amanda. This is the only way."

I thought of Supersize, falling from the sky, screaming on the way down. He'd never have tried that climb if it weren't for Diesel. And maybe I'd be taking Jo up on her offer to return the favor sooner than she expected.

"Okay, I'll help you. What's the plan?"

Jo filled me in, and I had to admit, her strategy was solid. Something about her desperation had me uttering words I never thought would leave my lips. "Look, Jo, if you ever need somewhere to crash, I have a safe place. A houseboat at the marina. It's yours if you need it." I ended the call before Jo could deflect my offer with one of her witty comebacks.

I was filled with renewed resolve. Like Jo, I'd do whatever it took to get vengeance. If it meant cashing in on a few favors, so be it.

Kat had risked a lot to tell me about Diesel. What if I hadn't believed her?

At least I wasn't the only one who saw through Diesel's facade. Were she and I enough to make a difference? Maybe not. A crazy plan began to form in my mind. Diesel had to be exposed.

No more death.

No more lies.

And just maybe the skills Diesel used me for would ultimately take him down.

From the inside out.

I took out my cell phone and started tracking down everything I could find about a school called Bishops Prep.

NINE

Jo had been bouncing around like she'd sucked back a flat of energy drinks at the prospect of a different disguise. But the moment we set foot on the golf-green grounds of Bishops Prep the day after our enlightening phone call, she flatlined.

If I had to go in alone, so be it. I could work some razzle-dazzle on the general nerd masses, but something told me having Jo present would bring swift results from our mark. She paused at the imposing double doors granting entry to the illustrious Bishops Prep.

I nudged her shoulder. "You okay?"

"Yeah," she squeaked out. "I'm fine."

Yeah right."

"We gonna do this?"

Oh, now she was going all gangsta. I choked back a laugh and scanned the text again. "Let's go. Security patrols the halls every fifteen minutes."

"That's what the student IDs are for."

My lips twisted. This wasn't as simple as making a fake ID to go clubbing. Any kid with a hacked copy of Photoshop could do that. Bishops Prep ID cards used embedded-chip technology. Students swiped them through specific access points—zones I'd researched and intended to avoid. The school had a reputation to uphold. Some of the country's richest families trusted the cards to keep their darling brats safe and sound. Protected from abduction attempts, terrorist activity and unwanted pregnancies. Yet Jo wanted to walk boldly inside and put her forgeries to the test.

"I know what I'm doing," she said. "The IDs will pass inspection."

If they didn't, alarms would trip ~
we'd be on the run from the school's version
of Homeland Security. "They catch us and
these uniforms won't help," I said.

I shouldn't have brought our current
wardrobe to Jo's attention. While I was
channeling my inner naughty Catholic
schoolgirl, Jo pulled at the short gray
skirt, white shirt and red tie, looking as
comfortable as a priest in drag.

"Wish I could wear my regular clothes,"
she said.

"We have to blend in or security will
kick us out for sure." I watched as she
tugged at the hemline of her skirt. "Stop
it." I jabbed her ribs with my elbow.
"You're going to get us caught."

Seriously, the girl had nothing to
worry about. Her ensemble suited her
just fine—in fact, our mark just might
melt in a pool of saliva at her feet. "You
clean up nice," I said.

I didn't have time to nurse Jo along.
That had been my mistake with Supersize—

ng things too slow. Not allowing him
o trust his own abilities. We had to move.
I put a hand to her back and pressed her
forward. "Go."

Inside, I sucked in a few deep breaths,
light-headed until my system adjusted.
I had called on a friend to do some research.
Big Bang—as he called himself—went to a
cross-town private school and was only too
happy to get me what I needed. His research
had told us about some of the unusual perks
at Bishops Prep. Like the crazy security and
the enhanced air—an infusion of oxygen
and nitrogen. And whoa. This place packed
a punch. But our only choice was to meet
with Jo's mark face-to-face. She'd tried
a few times, and he kept giving her the
brush-off. Time to help Jo stand out and
get noticed. Jo was used to staying in the
background, but today I was pushing her
out of her comfort zone and into the world
of dude-you-can't-avoid-me-any-longer.

Jo took a few moments to steady herself,
but finally she met my gaze. Her eyes were

sort of glazed over. Time to rip off
Band-Aid. "You going to stand there c
work?" I needed her sharp.

My harsh tone seemed to snap her out
of it. "Let's go," she said.

I skimmed the text once more. "He
should be in a part of the cafeteria called
Lounge A. Down the hall, to the left."
I fired her a glare. She was such a newbie.

We slipped down the hall and arrived
at the cafeteria. For the socially awkward,
it was the equivalent of the scary basement
in every horror movie ever made. Jo looked
about to lose it. "You need a minute?"

"No," she gasped.

"Let's go."

We weaved through the crowd. I spotted
a few banners mounted on the walls.
They weren't for the usual football and
basketball championships, but for year
after year of zone and provincial rankings
in brainiac events like robotics, chess
tournaments, young inventors. No wonder
Big Bang hadn't had to do much digging

et me the information I'd needed
out Bishops Prep's security and layout.
I'd asked him for information about his
school's fiercest competition. He probably
had backup servers filled with all kinds
of obscure details.

"See him?" Jo's voice, low and tense.

I frowned and eyed the largest throng
of kids gathered around a few tables. We
were close—I knew it. "Go right. I'll go
left. He's got to be here."

We spotted him at the same time.
He was staring down some nerdling
over a chessboard, surrounded by card-
carrying members of the four-eyes club.
I'd never seen so many spectacles outside
an optical store.

Jo's nerves were getting the better
of her. "How do you want to play this?"
she asked as I moved up beside her.

I grinned. "Bond him."

Jo blinked. "Bond?"

"James Bond." I shrugged. "Bond-girl
him."

"You think that'll work?"

"He's a guy, isn't he?"

"Yeah, I guess." She sounded uncertain.

"You go left, I'll go right. Angel and devil. Got it?"

She frowned. "Like good girl, bad girl?"

I laughed. "More like bad Bond girl"—I jerked a thumb in her direction—"and badder Bond girl"—I pointed both thumbs at myself.

We parted ways, and I moved through the crowd, sexing it up for the boys with a bit of sass to my stride. They ate it up. I grinned back at them.

We flanked Jace, closing in on him in unison.

I put my hand on his right shoulder. Jo did the same to his left. A hush settled over the crowd, and an audible gulp came from the kid across the table.

I bent close, pretending to whisper sweet nothings into his ear.

And let him have it.

"Well, hello there, Clark Kent...I mean Jace. It's your two-for-one package deal of kryptonite dropping in for a little 3-D face time." While he barely spared me a glance, his eyes flickered with awareness as Jo shoved her chest into his shoulder. She was really pulling out all the stops, managing to do more than look the part. I think she was actually getting into it. She too began to whisper in Jace's ear, draping her body around his like a second skin. For a girl who spent most of her time dressed as a boy, she had some serious moves.

Frankly, I was impressed.

So was Jace's opponent, who appeared to be struggling to breathe, his eyes nearly popping from his skull as he watched us from across the board. He dropped his white knight in a kamikaze move that made me cringe.

"Sorry to interrupt your little game," I told Jace. "I know you probably wanted to win fair and square. Isn't it amazing the damage a bit of girl power can do?"

I let out a low laugh for the gaping crowd. Jace barely noticed. He kept giving Jo furtive glances when she turned her head away. "Jo thinks you're some kind of kindred spirit," I said. "She might even be interested in you. And you'd like that. I can tell. We both know *I'm* not the one getting you hot and bothered right now."

His gaze met Jo's for a long moment. While he was distracted, I swiped one of his fallen rooks from the edge of the table.

"She's a sweet kid," I continued, smiling now that I had the advantage. Jace's eyes narrowed. He could tell I was up to something. "So you just sit there and hear her out, or I will slip one of your captured pieces on the board and get you disqualified for cheating."

TEN

We left Bishops Prep with a deal on the table. Jace would get the goods for Jo, and he'd also help me. Jo took the deal at face value, but then, she was new to such negotiations, and I'd been navigating around Diesel for years. If we were going to be putting our lives on the line, I needed more dirt on Jace. The guy with his little hacker friend, Bentley, was a giant mystery box I had to crack open.

Later that night I scaled the wrought-iron fence that surrounded the Wyatt property. It was one thing to get Jo on Jace's radar, but Diesel had taught me well.

I didn't do anything for anyone if there wasn't something in it for me. And what I wanted Jace for was personal—I hadn't let Jo in on the fact that I had more than helping her in mind when I acted as her wingman.

The last thing I needed was her asking a million questions and getting in my face when it was her own neck she should be worrying about. I couldn't stomach the thought of another innocent kid getting mixed up in this mess. And possibly getting seriously hurt. Jace and his hacker were another breed—one I could relate to—flawed and more of the criminal persuasion. We knew what we were getting into and accepted the risks.

I began my descent, mindful of the security cameras dotting the fenceposts. I'd reached the side door to the four-car garage and was just about to start working on the lock when a deep voice cut through the night.

"Stop right there. I have a gun."

I started to hold up my hands, then laughed and dropped them to my hips. "No you don't. Anyone with a gun doesn't need to announce to the world that he has one." I spun to face Jace. He stood on the driveway, still wearing his prep-school uniform. He held a broom like he was about to crack a home run with the mother of all dust balls—my head.

I squinted at the broom.

Jace squinted at me, and recognition slid over his face, like he'd spotted a spider on the floor. One he thought he'd already stomped on. "Oh, it's you."

"Roll out the welcome wagon, why don't you. Wait a minute." I let out another laugh. "Is that a freaking *Quidditch* broom?" I put my hands back up in the air. "I come in peace. No need to bring out the magic."

Jace stared at the makeshift weapon in his hands. He tossed the broom aside. Its bristles caught on the manicured bushes lining the driveway, and the broom dangled a few feet off the ground.

Like maybe it did have the power of flight.

"That's not mine." He crossed his arms defensively across his chest.

"Ri-ight," I drawled.

"What are you doing here? No one has this address."

"That's not exactly true. Your school records say you're living in the penthouse suite of a high-rise downtown, and yet it sits practically empty. *This* place, where you spend most of your time when you're not strong-arming your way through a chess game, was a bit tougher to find, but not mission impossible." I smiled.

Jace smiled back. "That would be really great, if my home were some secret fortress of solitude. But it's just a house."

"A really big, gigantic house that you were trying to keep a secret. I think that qualifies."

A scowl replaced Jace's smile. "I don't know what you want, but I'm not interested. Get the hell off my property." He turned on his heel and started for the house. His easy dismissal of me had my back up.

I got down to business.

"Someone I cared about died. But he's dead, and I'll never see him again. And the worst thing is…it was my fault." My voice was soft, but my words hit Jace like a hook snags a fish. Reeling him in. His steps slowed. He turned to face me. Walked back toward me until only a few feet separated us. "I told him to trust a man the way I did. Blindly. The man—Diesel—was like a father to me. To them. But it was all a lie."

"I know what it's like to be lied to." Jace's fists clenched at his sides.

"I thought you might."

"So what do you want to do about it?"

"There are others like me, kids who put their faith in Diesel. They need to know what he really is. That's what I want. Him. Exposed." I held out the list I'd prepared. "These are the few who made it out." I gave a low laugh. "Or so he said. He set them free, let them lead normal lives, and they never looked back." I swallowed hard. "I need to know they're safe. I've given you everything I know about them. What they let slip about their lives before, bits of their real names, real lives. If you and your hacker friend could find them…"

Jace stuffed the handwritten list in his pocket. "We'll try."

"I can pay you. I have money saved."

"I don't want your money." Jace's lips twisted. "But you *will* owe me."

I nodded. After seeing his digs, I knew Jace wouldn't come cheap. I'd expected a trade of services. "Of course."

He turned and made again for his home.

"What makes Jo think she can trust you?" My words froze him in place, but he didn't turn back around.

"I don't know." He glanced over his shoulder. His eyes glittered in the night. "What makes her think she can trust *you*?" He continued across the lawn.

Good question.

I glanced around at the huge expanse of ground, the multiple levels leading down to a boathouse, a dock and the glorious waterfront, then took in the imposing two-story brick home. The high fence and automatic gate. Something was off.

Then I got it. The absolute silence.

No one had come out to check on Jace or back him up when he'd gone charging after an intruder, armed with only a wizard's broom. Not hired security or his parents. Except for Jace, the place was just a sprawling *Better Homes and Gardens* isolation tank he called home. At the warehouse, I was constantly surrounded by people, and yet I felt just as alone as Jace looked right now, striding across the lawn to enter an empty house. I wondered where his family was.

Just as alone as Jo had been for who knows how long before she'd reached out to me. But each of us had taken on the responsibility of protecting or avenging those few who had become dear to us. Willing to risk our lives to see justice done. We were all so different and yet so much the same.

A smile tugged at my lips. Maybe some of his embrace-your-inner-nerd, T-shirt-wearing, comic-loving, see-the-world-through-superhero-colored-glasses world view had seeped into my veins, but Supersize would say we were like Dark Knights. Tarnished warriors out to take on the big bads with a bit of beauty, brawn and brains.

Jace could have called the cops when he spotted me. He could have said no to Jo and me, could have said screw the consequences. And yet he agreed to help us both. He understood the need for vengeance.

The need for the truth to be exposed. I wondered what truth he was looking for.

I let out a long breath, tension easing from my shoulders, and the knot that had been coiling in my gut starting to loosen.

Sureness seeped into my bones. It was hard to admit I couldn't take Diesel down on my own. But even Batman had Robin. Now Jo, Jace, his friend and I were all indebted to each other. I thought of Supersize and his failed attempt to play the hero. I couldn't let his death be for nothing.

Some debts could never be paid.

"Hey," I called out to Jace's retreating form. "We're good, right? I need you guys for your wicked hacker skills and ability to knock down pawns. You know that, right?"

Jace dipped his head in agreement but didn't look back. He entered his house and closed the door behind him.

That went well, I thought.

ELEVEN

"And fare thee well, my only Luve
   And fare thee well, a while!
   And I will come again, my Luve,
   Tho' it were ten thousand mile."

The last bell screeched, drowning out Mr. Nicholson's recitation of Robert Burns's "A Red, Red Rose," complete with a thick Scottish brogue and a plastic rose pinned to his shirt pocket. Nicholson was all about the props.

Still, he'd managed to weave a spell over at least half the class. Girls blinked back to awareness while the guys rolled their eyes and bolted from the room.

Except for Emmett. His gaze lingered on mine as I weaved through the desks and made for the door.

The weight of his stare, the heat of it, left me gasping by the time I reached the safety of the hall. Since the debacle with the kiss of all kisses, Emmett had kept his distance. But he still looked at me. Driving me mad with those concerned, wanting, dark eyes. Eyes that saw more than most.

I lingered outside Nicholson's door. Emmett hadn't exited yet. I could slip back inside and...and what? Tell him I couldn't stop thinking about him? That I wished it was him who was taking me to that stupid freaking dance? That we'd have the most amazing time in the history of lame school dances? And I'd pick him up—in a car I'd stolen?

My cell phone thrummed in my pocket, making my decision for me. I answered the call and deliberately forced my steps toward the school's front foyer. Leaving

Emmett and his normal little life safely behind.

"It's Jace," a low voice said in my ear.

"How did you get this number?" I frowned. Jo might have given Jace hers, but I hadn't handed out any digits.

"You two came to me, remember?" Jace all but growled. "You wanted the best. Well, you got it."

I snorted. *Arrogant much?* I was infinitely glad Jo was the one stuck on him and not me. I had my own tall, dark and brooding to deal with. "I'm betting it was your hacker friend who landed my number. Bentley's the brain, you're the brawn." I paused. "Oh right. But you embrace your inner nerd with the chess thing. You're like a Renaissance man."

"I'll take that as a compliment. Are you still on for tonight?"

"Of course I am. I picked the location, remember? Robson and Burrard at midnight."

"Good."

He ended the call. I stared at my cell for a few seconds, then shook my head. Abrupt jerk. But there was a lightness to my step as I descended the stairs outside the school and headed for the bus. I might be risking a lot by helping Jo tonight, but I wasn't doing it alone.

* * *

At exactly 12:15 AM, I couldn't take it anymore.

"Will you stop with the pacing?" I smacked Jace's arm as he crossed in front of me. "You're making me nervous. What does it matter if Jo's late? Bentley is AWOL too."

"He isn't AWOL. He's waiting for us at another location." I must have looked as pissed as I felt, because he held up a hand. "Don't start. No, that wasn't part of the plan. But I wanted to be sure Jo got here safe with no one following her before we picked up Bentley."

So Jo and I weren't the only ones with trust issues. I kind of respected Jace for that.

Jace glanced at his cell. "Something's wrong. She should be here by now." He plugged in a few numbers, then spoke into the phone. "Track Jo's cell."

I held my breath. Right. If Jace's friend had our phone numbers, hacking into the phone-company servers and accessing the tracking software would be a breeze. You know, for a genius and all that. A short time later, Jace said a terse "Thanks, we'll pick you up in five" into the phone, and then he was dragging me along to his SUV.

"What's going on? Where are we going?" I opened the passenger door, but Jace jerked his head.

"Backseat. Bentley sits there."

"Are you serious?" I griped, hopping in behind the passenger seat, as far away from Jace as possible. The guy was on my last nerve.

He peeled away from the curb. "As to where we're going, we're going after Jo, of course. Bentley has her location. She's on the move, and it's not in our direction. It will be easier if he's here to navigate."

We pulled up in front of a Dairy Queen. Jace went inside, telling me to "stay put" like I was an untrained puppy. Less than a minute later he exited with his friend. Shorter than Jace. Much shorter. As in dwarf shorter. He had a high forehead and a very chopped walking stride. He wore a backpack slung over his shoulder, and he was chowing down on a Peanut Buster Parfait with a look of absolute bliss on his face.

"Bentley, this is Raven. Raven, Bentley." Jace introduced us as he pulled the SUV back into traffic.

"Mhuufff…" Bentley said around a mouthful of goopy ice cream.

I met Jace's gaze in the rearview mirror. This explained much. Jace kept Bentley tucked away because he was different—but with his talents and lack of social skills, so easy to exploit. No wonder

Jace played guard dog.

Jace plucked the icy treat from Bentley's grip, lowered the driver's-side window and tossed it out. "Time to focus, Bentley," he said. "Where's Jo now?"

Bentley shrugged. He pulled out a tablet from his backpack, accessed an application and pointed left. "That way. The signal is stationary. It has settled in one location. Close now." Silence for a few blocks, then another finger point. "That way."

And so it went until we turned onto a dark residential street. We rounded a corner. A chemical scent drifted in through the car vents. I wrinkled my nose.

"Where is she, Bentley?" Jace's voice was deadly calm. "Where's Jo?"

Bentley panicked, twisting in his seat. He held a hand to his mouth, muffling his words, but when I made them out, they filled me with absolute dread.

"She's inside the fire." He pointed to a house straight ahead that looked as abandoned as the other houses around it.

But something churned behind the front window. I squinted into the night.

Smoke. That's what the smell was.

"This is so not good." I shoved my door open, but Jace was already out of the SUV.

He stopped me with a curse and a solid grip on my forearm. "I'm stronger than you—I can carry her out of there. You can't."

"You're not Superman. What if you need help clearing a path? Or finding the exit? I'm coming with you."

"Me too," Bentley said, standing beside me.

Jace scowled, his features set in hard lines. He fired me a killer glance. "If it gets too dangerous, you come back to the car with Bentley, understood? Don't let him out of your sight."

"I won't."

The three of us bolted for the house. I was surprised at Bentley's speed. The back entrance seemed the least affected by the fire. "Must have started near the living room," I said.

We navigated through the derelict interior, rats streaming by us in their panic to escape. The smoke was worse in the narrow hallway. Here, Bentley had the height advantage. He was low, and the smoke didn't hit his face like it did ours. I hunched over. Jace followed suit, and we half crawled into the living room.

There. Jo had been tied to a column between the living room and the small galley kitchen. Jace cursed under his breath, charging forward. He held a hand to Jo's face, and she began to cough.

I took the pocketknife I kept strapped to my ankle and cut the plastic ties that bound Jo's wrists to the column. "Newb," I said when Jo's bloodshot eyes met mine.

Jace hoisted Jo over his shoulder. "Idiot," he said.

We followed him out, Bentley trailing close behind me. The house continued to burn as we hoofed it to the SUV.

"Jerks," Jo countered weakly once we were outside and the fresh air hit our lungs. "You tracked the laptop GPS. You were supposed to put the files on the Internet."

Jace said something back to Jo, but I couldn't make out the words. Then he got louder. "We're a team, whether you like it or not." He placed her gently in the backseat.

Jo's head swiveled around. "God, how many cars do you have?" she asked.

"Wait till you see the clubhouse," I said, thinking of Jace's estate. I didn't think Jo heard me—she closed her eyes in exhaustion.

"Should we take her to the hospital?" The words had barely left my lips when Jo's eyes opened wide.

"No way! I'm fine. Just get me out of here."

I climbed in beside her and kept checking on her during the trip. We soon arrived at Jace's estate, the iron gate swinging smoothly open as we entered the driveway.

Jo tried to make the walk to the house under her own steam, but Jace would have none of it. I tried not to be dazzled as he carried her into the house via an entrance within the four-car garage. I also tried not to think about the price I could get for the vehicles tucked safely inside. Diesel would have a conniption if he saw the cherry-red vintage 1930s Ford Coupe. A car in that condition... maybe sixty grand.

Plus it just looked really cool.

Jace set Jo down on a leather sofa in what had to be the biggest living room I'd ever seen. And the sparsest. No books lying around, no half-eaten bags of chips. Like one of those grand show homes you could buy tickets for at the exhibition. The place just didn't look lived in.

While Jace cleaned up Jo's scrapes, I hovered over Bentley's shoulder as he accessed the files on the laptop Jo had provided. Holy hell, the guy was efficient. Stubby fingers, but those fingers moved like lightning. My gaze fixed on a tattoo on his inner wrist. Interesting. I'd never have pegged Bentley as an ink man, but the small, black infinity symbol seemed to suit him. Mathish. Hackerish.

The screen flooded with text, demanding my attention. At first it meant nothing, but then a picture began to form.

"Payments," I said, finally getting what Jo's corrupt cop had been up to. "Looks like she was helping someone hide drug shipments and avoid any raids."

"There's more," Jo said. "I don't know what it is, but it goes beyond drugs." She rose up on her elbows. "What now? Upload the files to the news outlets? Take it to a police station and hope some cop listens?"

Jace shot her a look. "You're kidding, right?" He took the laptop from Bentley. "We send it directly to the police chief." Jo moved over to Jace and the laptop and typed something. Then Jace hit *Send*.

A happy *bing* told us an email had been sent.

"There *are* benefits to being a member of one of Vancouver's most powerful families," Jace said with a sarcastic grin.

I shook my head. "Figures you'd know him."

Stretching, I embraced the feeling of one small victory for the little guy, courtesy of, well, the little guy and all present company. Still, I felt the need to reinforce just exactly how things stood between Jo and me. And that was a simple exchange of services. "I helped you. Remember that when I come calling in the favor."

TWELVE

That day came much sooner than I expected. It was a few days after we'd rescued Jo, and she and I were getting along well. She was living on the boat, and I was still flying high after working with Jace and Bentley—who, it turned out, was Jace's brother—to save her. Things had been set in motion. We'd helped to do some good and give Jo closure. It was a good feeling, but there was still a lot of work to be done.

I lost myself in music during the bus trip home from school. Hopping off at a nearby stop, I hoofed it the rest of the way—about six blocks through industrial buildings until I reached the warehouse. All of us were trained to change up our routes to our illegal little home base.

Establish a pattern and eventually someone will notice.

My grief over Supersize lingered, but in the distance. Like my mixed-up feelings about Emmett. I'd managed to tamp those things down and fill the gap with plans for revenge. Diesel's betrayal had gutted me, and I'd put myself back together the only way I knew how. The same way I'd managed to walk away from my parents and adapt to life in the ring. I was in survival mode. The force of it put sort of a shield around me, cutting off the pain and nurturing the anger.

For the moment I was simply thrilled that my plan had been set into motion. With Jo, Jace and Bentley on my side, I knew the end was in sight. Hadn't we just toppled one of the city's most corrupt cops?

Go us.

I had little time to celebrate, though, as mass chaos greeted me the moment I arrived at the warehouse that afternoon. About ten of the fifteen kids living at the warehouse, along with most of the chop-shop guys, milled around in little groups. Gesturing wildly with their hands. Talking loud enough for me to hear them over the guitars squealing in my ears.

When they noticed I'd entered via the side door, they bolted for me like zombies on fresh meat.

I popped out my earbuds and was soon overwhelmed by the clamor, the chorus of voices echoing to the rafters. When I'd left that morning, no one would talk to me. Now no one would stop.

"Did you hear about Kat?"

"So glad you're back—we thought they had you too."

"Diesel's been losing his mind. You know he has us on lockdown?"

What did they mean, *lockdown?*

"Guys, calm down." I held up a hand, and gradually they quieted down. "What happened with Kat? I have no idea what you're talking about." Where was Link? Didn't he know there was practically a mutiny going on?

As if reading my thoughts, Link's gruff growl sliced across the warehouse. "Raven, about time you showed up," he called from his ground-level office just beyond the hydraulic lifts used to hoist the cars for easy dismantling. Even from this distance, I could tell he was good and pissed. He crooked his finger. "We gotta talk." The same finger jabbed in the air at the kids milling around. "Everyone else, get back to work." He strode into his office, leaving the door open for me to follow.

I felt the stares of everyone as I entered the office and closed the door on their disgruntled faces. In the muffled quiet of Link's office, I watched as he paced the narrow room. I leaned my back against the door. Waiting. I'd learned over the years that Link would talk when he was good and ready. Push too hard, too fast, and he just clammed up.

Not what I wanted.

Finally he found his words. "Diesel sent a group out on another run. I told him it was too soon after Supersize, that no one's head was in the game, but you know how he's been."

Boy, did I. I nodded.

"Kat got sloppy. She was picked up by the cops."

I swore under my breath. So much for getting her in on my plan.

"Diesel is at his paranoid best. Now that you're back, the warehouse is officially on lockdown."

"What does that even mean?"

Link shrugged. "Just what you probably think it means. The police force will be hunting down all the car jockies they can track. No one comes in or out, unless it's to do a job."

"For how long?" Crap. While I'd been focused on staying out of Diesel's way, things around the warehouse had been steadily getting worse. I'd been in denial, really, hanging out with Jo at the houseboat, helping her adjust to life with a semipermanent roof over her head. I kept thinking she'd take off at any moment and head back to the streets, but the girl was smart. She knew when to lie low.

In her case, it was the right move. In mine? Not so much. Avoiding the warehouse seemed to have only made things worse.

"Until his cops say the pressure's off. Until we know Kat hasn't talked. We don't want anyone to put her together with Supersize. Right now, the cops have declared his death an accident. But we can't have any more incidents like that."

Incident, right. Diesel had to pay.

But how could I put my plan into act' if I couldn't even leave the warehous'

I slapped my hands on my thighs. "But what about school? I'm not the only one who goes. The semester is almost over. I have exams…"

"You'll catch up. You always do. And trust me, the others don't care as much. You're the only one stressing over school."

"Maybe. But did you see them out there?" I gestured at the door. "They're ready to bolt, Link. You can't keep us trapped in here. We're not rats in a cage."

"You don't get it, Raven." Link grabbed my arms and gave me a shake. "There's more at stake than you know. I need you to get those kids under control. Work on them until you get them to sit tight and I can get Diesel to ease up. Talk to them— they trust you."

" right." I let out a huff. "After
…th…" I couldn't even
ud. "They blame me,
loes. Everyone turned
you."

"No, you're wrong." Link's jaw worked. "We were shocked, that's all. Couldn't believe what Diesel was trying to pull. Pointing the finger at you when we knew exactly who sent the kid on a suicide mission. I tried to tell them, but they won't listen to me. They'll do what you say. I'll try to keep the heat off you, but if—"

A knock at the door interrupted whatever Link had been about to say. He released me just as the door opened.

Diesel's goons—or, as I called them, since Diesel had never offered their names, Thing 1 and Thing 2—stood in the doorway. "Is there a problem?"

"Not at all, my friends. Just filling Raven in on the situation." Link gave me a push. "Well, get a move on, girl." He gave me a steely look. "You know what to do."

I sucked in a slow breath. Coming to terms with this new reality. I should have left and sailed away on *Big Daddy* when I had the chance. This haven, our hom had become a prison. And I had to talk everyone into accepting it.

Standing in the middle of the warehouse with Diesel's goons at my back and every kid in the place sneaking glances at me, looking for guidance, I hoped Link hadn't seriously overestimated my powers of persuasion. Because I'd rally the troops, all right. But I wasn't planning on encouraging them to blindly follow Diesel's orders.

Not anymore.

THIRTEEN

That night I stealthily made the rounds of the warehouse's sleeping quarters and talked to those I knew had their doubts about Diesel or had been on the wrong side of his temper before, enlisting their help. My plan was simple. They'd stage a revolt—attack Thing 1 and Thing 2 and cause a mess for Diesel to deal with—and I'd use the opportunity to break into his office. I didn't get into the specifics of what I would be doing once inside, but I told them the truth.

If they kept the office clear for at least ten minutes, I could put an end to Diesel, and no one in the warehouse would have to suffer under his rule. Not ever again.

Of course, that meant the warehouse would be fodder for the cops.

We'd lose our home. The protection Diesel's name provided. The jobs that kept us fed. We were giving up everything to take back our freedom. Some of the kids would just end up back in another car-theft ring, or worse. But some would seize the moment and try to turn their lives around.

Diesel had been a generous leader once. Everyone agreed it wasn't safe working under him any longer. He was a danger to anyone he recruited. If we could take him down, maybe our sacrifices would save the life of some unknown kid like Supersize.

By morning, the plan was set.

I sat on my cot, bleary-eyed. My stomach churned. This was the day that would either make me or break me.

I grabbed my cell. Called Jo.

"It's six in the morning," she groaned.

"And you've been sleeping on my houseboat for free. Did you water Charlie?"

"Yes, I watered your plant. Although I'm pretty sure it's just a dandelion."

"It's a begonia, and don't you dare kill it." I paused, swiped a hand down my face. She didn't say anything. "You still there?"

"Yeah, what do you want?"

"Look, I called to ask you..." My vision blurred. I cleared my throat. "I need to call in that favor."

A rustle of movement. "Now?"

"Well, not now, but tonight. Is that a problem?"

"No. I mean, I never thought you'd actually admit you needed—I mean, for sure. I'm there. How can I help?"

I was used to doing things for other people. Now I was putting my faith in Jo, Jace and Bentley to the test. Had they only been using me? Or were we really a team?

I guessed I was about to find out.

"Diesel, my boss, put the warehouse on lockdown." I filled Jo in on the details. "I've gotten everyone on board. They'll do their part. I need you to go to my school, Laurier Secondary, and talk to a guy for me. I don't have his number, and this isn't something I can ask him over the phone."

"A gu-uy," Jo echoed, dragging the word out so it had at least three syllables. "Just a guy, or is he *your* guy?"

I let out a groan. "He's just a guy, okay? I need you to ask him if he'll do one thing for me. I need his father to be here at the warehouse tonight. At 9:00 PM sharp. Emmett is absolutely not to come on his own. Just his father. Tell him it's about the note he gave me. It's my reply. He'll understand."

"You want his father there? Not him? ˙ ˙ get it."

˙ cop."

ıardened. "Ask Jace."

ısking Jace and Bentley

in another department

more worthy of their skills. Besides, I can't send Jace to ask Emmett to help me—that will just set him off." It would play out way better if a girl did the asking, and when Jo wanted to, she had enough charm to mesmerize a shark. She'd caught Jace's eye, hadn't she?

"Ah, you mean Jace would make him jealous. So he *is* yours."

"Jo, can you do this for me or not? I know you have issues with cops. So do I. But I had some friends look into Emmett's dad, and if I'm going to trust a uniform... he's the best bet." That was true. Out of curiosity, I'd done a little digging, and there was nothing to suggest Emmett's dad was sketchy in any way. In fact, the word around school was he'd declined a promotion and a pay raise just so Emmett wouldn't have to change schools during his senior year. Hardly the MO of a cop on the take.

Finally, after much coaxing, Jo agreed. I told her which classes Emmett had sad that I knew his schedule as well as my own. I was going to call Jace next, but a knock at my door had me stowing my cell phone under my pillow. I dove back under my scratchy woolen blanket.

"Yeah, I'm up," I called out, adding a sleepy tone to my voice.

Diesel entered, alone for once.

While I wouldn't have felt any safer if he'd come in with Thing 1 and Thing 2 behind him, it did make me question why he'd decided to seek me out in my room.

I sat up, pulling the blanket tight to my chest, wishing I'd worn more than a tank top and shorts to bed. A jolt of fear stabbed up my spine. My heart pounded like a jackhammer. Diesel never came near the sleeping quarters. And now he sat at the end of my cot.

Rested a heavy hand on my feet under the blanket.

Stared at me with assessing eyes, as if he wondered how far he could go before

I'd been scared by Diesel before. By his anger. His mood swings and snap judgments. His faulty decision making.

But never like this.

"Happy birthday, Raven," he said, shattering the silence that had gone on too long and been full of weirdness. He snapped his wrist, causing me to flinch, but I recovered in time to see that he'd tossed me something.

I grabbed it, turning the present over in my hands.

"Open it." Something in his voice had the hair at the back of my neck standing on end. I lifted the lid of a small, plainly wrapped box about two inches wide and three inches deep. I gasped as I removed a delicate glass object from the tissue paper inside.

Light glittered on the intricate twists and details of a black raven trapped within a golden birdcage.

A symbol of my captivity. But cages begged to be busted wide open. Funny h

Diesel intended to threaten me with his little gift, but he'd only strengthened my resolve. He should know symbols meant different things to different people.

I thought of Bentley's tattoo. To him, I was sure it represented more than his love of computers. It probably symbolized hope or that life was one endless stream of possibilities. Sure, that worked on a certain level. But to me those seamlessly linked loops meant something entirely different—what goes around, comes around. My fist clenched around the caged bird in my hand.

When I looked up, Diesel was gone.

I knew he'd sent Supersize after the impossible. He knew my untried apprentice wouldn't make the climb to the top of the parkade. He'd counted on it. Supersize had died because Diesel wasn't *ever* going to let me go.

FOURTEEN

At 8:50 PM on my sixteenth birthday,
all hell broke loose. Kids stormed
the lower level of the warehouse and
began smashing car parts and releasing
engine hoists, cheering when the heavy
machinery smashed to the concrete floor.
Thing 1 and Thing 2 split up to try to
break the kids into smaller groups, only to
find themselves ducking from wrenches,
power tools, spark plugs—anything that
could be launched in their direction.

While they struggled against an angry
mob of close to twenty teens, I crept up
to Diesel's office. Diesel was gone and
missing all the action. Another late-night

meeting with the people who pulled his strings. Disappointment gnawed at me, but it was now or never. Diesel might not be on the grounds when Emmett's dad arrived but this was a chance I had to take.

Maybe they'd be able to track him down. Maybe, but I doubted it.

Still, he'd never be able to return to *this* warehouse, or screw up the lives of *these* kids, and that had to count for something.

Footsteps pounded up the stairs. Too heavy to be one of the kids. Had to be one of the goons.

A few quick steps and I hid in the closet to the left of and slightly behind Diesel's desk. The office door creaked open. Footsteps approached. Slow and steady, circling the room. Whoever it was, he wasn't here to hide. He was looking for someone.

"Raven?" a low voice whispered.

He was looking for me.

Carefully I shifted to the far corner of the closet. I reached both hands out at shoulder height and hopped off the ground. Then, with my hands and feet braced against the wall, I began to climb, ninja style. Soon I was suspended about four feet high, clinging to the walls to keep myself aloft.

When the closet door burst open, I was not in plain view. A man's arm reached in, riffled through some of Diesel's shirts and suit coats. Then the closet door slammed shut. My upper arms and quads trembled with the strain. It got harder to control my breathing.

After a long moment of silence, the footsteps retreated. The office door creaked shut. I waited a full minute more, just to be safe, then dropped to the floor with a groan. I exited the closet—and came to a complete stop.

Link stood in front of me, his arms folded across his chest.

"I knew you'd be in here." He gestured to the destruction unfolding in the bay below. "This wasn't what I had in mind when I spoke with you yesterday."

"No, I suppose not." I walked to the desk, fighting the urge to ask Link for his help. I knew he had a soft spot for me... but then, I'd thought the same thing about Diesel. None of them could be trusted.

I turned on Diesel's laptop and inserted a USB drive. "But you won't stop me, because you know Diesel's out of control. He had Supersize killed, Link. You know why, don't you?"

The burly man looked away.

"It was the same with Kat, wasn't it?" A flash of inspiration. I knew I was onto something. "She was a few months from her birthday too. We're the first to age out in, like, forever. She didn't screw up that night." I let out a breath. "She let herself get caught. Prison was better than whatever Diesel had planned." I slammed my fist on the desk.

typist at the best of times. "Okay, enter this user name and password…"

I did as instructed. And presto, Bentley had full access to Diesel's laptop.

I watched as the laptop seemingly took on a life of its own. Documents opened and closed, and folders were both uploaded and saved to the USB drive. Every dirty deal Diesel had ever made.

It was done.

Now all I had to do was get out of the warehouse.

FIFTEEN

From my perch on the window ledge outside Diesel's office I had a clear view of kids running out the side exit. That had been one of my conditions when I proposed this crazy plan. They were to cause a freaking riot, do as much damage as they wanted, leave Diesel's goons incapacitated but relatively unharmed, then get out by nine.

I scaled the wall to the roof and ran toward the wing of the warehouse that backed onto the alley where I'd had Jace leave one of his cars for me to make a quick exit.

Not the '30s Ford Coupe, though I'd asked for it. Repeatedly.

Throwing a leg over the ledge, I quickly climbed down to the alley.

Headlights snapped on, freezing me in place. I held up a hand to block the light. Doors opened, and two dark silhouettes approached.

"Raven, my dear," came Diesel's voice from the left. Controlled. No, enraged. "I suspected I'd find you back here. Running away, are we?"

A hand snatched my arm in a fierce grip. Not Diesel's. Wheels's. Diesel had always said Wheels did "odd jobs as required." I had always wondered what that had entailed.

"Don't you wish you really could fly now, little bird?" Wheels pulled me to his side, his hands groping and searching my flesh, checking me for a weapon. He neglected to check the boot where I stashed my pocketknife. That would be my last resort if Emmett's dad didn't get here soon. Where was he? It had to be past 9:00 PM. What if Jo had bailed on me? Hadn't even asked Emmett? I clenched my fist around the USB drive, my blood pumping from adrenaline and sheer terror.

"She's clean." Wheels threw me at Diesel, but my mentor, the man who'd practically been a father to me, didn't catch me.

He sidestepped, watching as my off-balance momentum drove me to the ground. My fingers spread wide, breaking my fall. Palms smashed into the concrete, the impact making me cry out. I lay there, stunned.

Diesel's polished black shoes came into view. As did the USB drive I'd dropped. He scooped it up from the ground. "Well, what do we have here?"

"Exactly what I was thinking," a man's voice said over a squawking PA system.

Another set of headlights snapped on, as did a swirling set of police lights.

"What the hell?" Diesel spun to face the officer, his face paling as he took in the two other cruisers pulling up.

I scrambled to my feet and ran. I reached Jace's car in record time, fired up the engine and shot out of sight. I drove about six blocks before I realized no one was following me. The cops had let me go. They had much bigger fish to fry.

I was free.

SIXTEEN

"You're sure I can stay? It'll only be a few more days, and then I'll have my own place."

I laughed at the earnestness in Jo's voice. "Stop stressing, will you? We're cramped on the boat, but we're safe. It's all good. It's better than good. It's fantastic. Just stop burning out my blow-dryer."

"That thing hates me. Okay, see you after school."

"You should be in school too, you know. Bentley can get you into any school you want. I hate to see that great mind going to waste."

"What great mind? Your blow-dryer has fried it already. No more school talk.

I told you guys I'd think about it. Between you and Bentley, I get a lecture every day." Jo laughed. "Wait a minute. Should *you* be in a class right now?"

"Busted." I grinned into the midday sky and ended the call. A flock of sparrows flittered by, coming to settle in a spruce tree beside the school. I sat on the school roof, watching their antics. I let my legs dangle over the edge and tapped my heels on the brick facade. The lightheartedness I'd felt while talking with Jo slipped away all too easily.

A week after my sixteenth birthday, and nothing was as I had imagined it would be.

The warehouse had been sectioned off as a crime-scene investigation. Diesel, Wheels and Thing 1 and Thing 2 had been taken into custody. They'd been exposed for what they were. Users. Men who preyed on the innocent.

The files we'd saved on the USB drive had also been emailed directly to the police chief. Who would probably set up another investigation to uncover who exactly had fed him information not once but twice in the space of a few weeks. Information that had led to the investigation of several members of city council, police officers and who knew who else.

I leaned back, raised my face to the sun and braced my weight with my hands.

Who would have thought a handful of kids could cause so much damage? Or do so much good? And we weren't done yet. Bentley had eliminated all traces of the warehouse kids from Diesel's files but had saved them for me. I was slowly working on the list of names. Tracking down the kids who'd left the warehouse. Some had moved out of the city, but a few were close by, and everything I feared about Diesel had come to light. These kids hadn't been set free; they'd just gone into other forms of servitude, trapped by guys like Diesel or worse.

If they'd accept my help, I would do all I could to get them out. So far, they'd just told me to get away as fast as I could and not look back. But I hadn't launched my houseboat yet. There were still things keeping me fixed in place.

I reached into my hoodie pocket and took out the glass raven Diesel had given me. Remembering everything it represented. I might be staying, but I wasn't caged. Not anymore. I stared at it for a few seconds, then fired the delicate ornament off the roof. It smashed to the ground and disintegrated into a fine dust.

A shadow blocked the sun. "Is that what you do when you come up here? Destroy things?"

Emmett stood over me. He approached slowly, one eye on me and the other on the drop to the school parking lot.

Stifling a laugh, I sat up and stared out at the day. Emmett sat beside me, slow and steady, as if every movement would send him over the edge. I guessed he hadn't scaled the wall like I had.

"Don't like heights?" I smirked.

"Hate them with a passion." Emmett's tone was conversational, casual, but his rapid breathing betrayed him. The guy was freaked, but he'd come after me anyway. I decided not to ride him too much.

"Found the ladder, did you?" I asked.

"Yeah."

We didn't speak for a while, just absorbed the day and the feeling of being close to each other.

"I guess you're waiting for me to say thank you." I shot him a look. "You didn't have to send your dad, but you did. You could have given him my name, but you didn't. So thank you."

He dipped his head. "You're welcome." He cautiously turned to face me. "I still have questions."

I nodded.

"And you're still not going to answer them."

I gave a slow smile as I shook my head. Nope, he'd get no answers from me. But I gave him something, at least. "If you want this to work, you just have to accept that there are some things I can't tell you."

"Or what? You'll have to kill me?"

I gave him a pointed stare. "It's not just me that's at risk. I'm not going to put you or anyone else in danger. Can you accept that?"

"For now." His eyes narrowed.

I braced myself for more. More questions. More demands.

Then he sighed. Relaxed. Got lost in the view. He seemed to get over his fear. A bit. "You know, this is amazing." We stared at the city and mountains in the distance. He linked his fingers with mine. I didn't pull away.

I did what I'd been scared to do before. I pulled him closer.

Our lips pressed together just as my cell phone thrummed the opening bass riff of an old song. I slapped my hand over my jeans pocket, muffling the sound.

Emmett let out a low laugh, his breath warm on my lips. "Are the '80s calling?"

I groaned. "That dude really is a lady. But she's really becoming a pain."

Emmett jerked his chin back. "What?"

Regretfully, I ran my finger over his bottom lip. "I have to get this. Give me five?"

"How about we meet back on solid ground?" Emmett stood, brushed off his jeans and backed slowly away from the edge of the roof.

"Wow," I said into my phone, watching Emmett head for the access ladder. "You are a real mood killer."

"All part of my charm." I heard the smile in Jo's voice. "Jace just called." There was a long pause.

"And…" I prompted into the silence.

"Annndd, he wants me, well, us…"

I laughed. "You tromped on my Emmett time to tell me something I figured out eons ago? Look, you like him. That's great. He likes you too. Just don't lose your head over him, Jo. You don't know anything about him. Not really."

"I know he needs our help." Her tone was all business. "It's his father. He's evil, and he needs to be stopped. We can help make that happen."

As she filled me in, any thoughts of razzing her about Jace completely slid from my mind.

Whoa.

My stomach rolled at the thought of what their father had put Bentley through.

Yes, the man had to be stopped.

I just hoped the guys were ready for the fallout, because if Jo and I were going to risk everything we'd just gotten back into our own hands—our lives, our freedom—we were going to make sure we had our backs covered.

I stared out at the afternoon sky and helped plot the downfall of one major evildoer.

What goes around, comes around.

ACKNOWLEDGMENTS

Special thanks to Sigmund and Natasha for creating such awesome characters, and three cheers to Andrew and the fantastic team at Orca.

Award-winning writer and screenwriter JUDITH GRAVES loves tragic romance, werewolves, vampires, magic and all things a bit creepy. A firm believer that teen fiction can be action-packed, snarky and yet hit all the right emotional notes, Judith writes stories with attitude. She lives in northern Alberta, and when she's not writing she works in a school library. For more information, visit www.judithgraves.com.

THE RETRIBUTION TRILOGY

A homeless kid on the run, a car thief who will
scale any height and a boxer with a secret life...
All seeking revenge on the adults who wronged them.
Reluctantly agreeing to become a team is the first step
in their hunt for RETRIBUTION.

A NEW HIGH-INTEREST YA TRILOGY THAT CAN BE READ IN ANY ORDER.

ORCA BOOK PUBLISHERS
www.orcabook.com • 1-800-210-5277

WWW.
RETRIBUTIONTHESERIES
.COM